The naughty step is right
at the bottom of the stairs. It's the place
where Sam has to sit if he ever behaves badly.

When Sam sits there,
he can't look at a book
or play with a toy.

All he can do
is think
and think
and think
about the naughty thing
he's done.

No one else in the house has to sit on the naughty step.

When Rover is naughty, he has to go to his basket.

When Nellie is naughty,
she has to go to her room.

And when Dad is naughty,
he has to sleep on the sofa.

So Sam **always** had the naughty step to himself, until . . .

. . . one
day,
with
a
loud
creeeaak,

someone else appeared.

"Who are you?" asked Sam, looking up at a shamefaced pirate, who sat down beside him.

"I'm Captain Buckleboots," he replied.
"And in case you're wondering why I'm here, I've been naughty . . .
very,
VERY
naughty."

"Oh dear," said Sam, "so have I."

Then the naughty step
gave another
creak . . .

"Jumping jellyfish!"
cried Captain Buckleboots.
"What's he doing here?"

"Have you been naughty too?"
Sam asked the little monster
who sat down to join them.

But before the monster could answer,
the step gave
two
more
creaks . . .

. . . and with the *swish* of a spacesuit
and the clunk of armor,
down sat an astronaut
and down sat a knight.

Suddenly the naughty step
was fuller than it had
ever been before.

So there they all sat
with nothing else to do
but **think** about
the naughty things
they'd done.

"I flew off in a RAGE," admitted the astronaut.

"And I was caught FIGHTING again,"
confessed the knight.

"And I behaved like a **LITTLE MONSTER**,"
said the little monster.

"G<small>RRR</small>RR!"

"How about you, Captain Buckleboots?" asked Sam. "What did you do?"

"Oh dear, oh dear, I behaved WORSE than all of you put together," blushed Captain Buckleboots.

"First, I picked on a pirate
smaller than me."

"That's **bad**,"
said the astronaut.

"Then I took something
that wasn't mine."

"That's **awful**,"
said the knight.

"Then I buried it in a place where he'd never be able to find it."

"How **monstrous**," said the monster.

"And, worst of all, when I was asked where it was, I said I didn't know."

"Oh dear," said Sam, "you've been **VERY** naughty."

"I know," sighed Captain Buckleboots. "How will I **ever** be forgiven?"

"Well . . ." said the astronaut, "when I
get off the naughty step, I'm going to give
everyone a **big hug** and say I'm **sorry**."

"And when I get off the naughty step," said the knight, "I'm going to **promise** not to fight anymore."

"And when I get off the naughty step, I'm going to be **sweet** and **kind** and not 'GRRRRR' so much," said the monster.

Captain Buckleboots thought hard for a moment.
"But because I've behaved SO badly," he said, "surely I'll need to do **something** even MORE **special** to be forgiven?"

"Well," said Sam, "you could write a **sorry note**."

"Jumping jellyfish!" exclaimed Captain Buckleboots. "What a terrific idea!"

"You can get OFF the naughty step now!" Sam's mother called from the kitchen.

"Good-bye, Sammy, my lad," said Captain Buckleboots. "Now I'm off to deliver this **very important letter**. Do you think I'll be forgiven?"

"Of course," said Sam. "If you **really mean it** when you say you're sorry, you're **sure** to be forgiven."

And, **jumping jellyfish**,
Sam was right!

the naughty step

Sam's house

Space station

dragon valley

So, at the end of a BUSY day on the naughty step, it was time for Sam to write a **Very Important Letter** of his own . . .

To mommy
I'm sorry
Love Sam x

. . . and because he **really**

REALLY meant it,
he was **sure** he'd be forgiven.

For Claire and Adi on
Howard Road — M.S.

For my nan and grandpa,
Marie and George — T.M.

First edition for the United States published in 2011 by Barron's Educational Series, Inc.
First published in the United Kingdom by Puffin Books Ltd. in 2010.
Text copyright © Mark Sperring, 2011
Illustrations copyright © Tom McLaughlin, 2011
The moral right of the author and illustrator has been asserted.
All inquiries should be addressed to: Barron's Educational Series, Inc.
250 Wireless Boulevard, Hauppauge, New York 11788
www.barronseduc.com
ISBN-13: 978-0-7641-4678-7   ISBN-10: 0-7641-4678-5
Library of Congress Catalog Card No. 2010931495
Date of Manufacture: November 2010
Manufactured by: South China Printing Co. Ltd., Guangdong, China
Printed in China
9 8 7 6 5 4 3 2 1